Gus and the JOY LIGHT

by Cheryl Bogardus

Illustrated by Mindy Stein

Inklet Press

Gus and the Joylight

We hope you enjoy this book from *Inklet Press*. Our goal is to produce high quality books that encourage, uplift and meet you where you are. We want our books to be fresh and creative. You will find other titles like this one and other books geared towards children and parents. *Inklet Press* titles may be purchased in bulk for educational, business, fundraising, sales or promotional use. For more information, please e-mail **info@inkletpress.com** or find us on Amazon as *Inklet Press* or go to our website: www.inkletpress.com.

Inklet Press
White Marsh, MD, USA
info@inkletpress.com

Published in White Marsh, Maryland, USA

To my husband, Harold, the best

friend I've ever had.

Gus and the JOY LIGHT

CHAPTER 1
The Awakening

When Gus opened his eyes for the very first time, it was already night. He lifted his head and saw thousands of stars twinkling, as if to say, "Hello!"

"Hello!" He called back.

A happy breeze came to play. It blew and twirled the fallen snow. Little snowflakes made light, lacy dances around his face. Then they sparkled away up into the sky.

"Oh! Is this what I *think* it is? Is this *life*?" Gus reached out his hands and touched the snowflakes. "How did this happen? I've been standing out in this

cold for so long and never once have I been able to feel it! And I could never say thank you for this fine cap or my handsome vest!"

Gus laughed and threw his head back so far his hat fell off. He opened his arms wide and sang up into the night sky. "This is the land of glistening snow, and I am a snowman! I'm a real, live snowman!" Then a little softer, "And this must be my home." Gus hopped and skipped through the snowy field. He was full of the fun and wonder of exploring someplace for the very first time.

After a while, dark clouds started to slide across the sky, covering the moon and stars. Gus didn't even notice. Or rather, he noticed something else. He could still see. In fact, he could see even better than before. There was a light coming out of him. He bent his head and opened his vest. There it was. Right over his heart. A soft, powerful glow that spelled JOY, made from perfectly ordinary stones!

"I remember now. There was a voice so gentle it felt like a puff of air on my face. It whispered, 'J...O...Y.' And I saw mittens. Beautiful red mittens pressed these stones into my snow, right there!

The voice said, 'You're complete now, Gus. You'll see.' So, I have a name! It's Gus! And I have joy. Real joy." Gus let out a loud "Woohoo! Woohoo!" He made tons of snowballs and stacked them almost as high as his nose. He ran crisscrossed paths through the snow until he was worn out. Then he threw himself on the ground and made snow angels. After a while, Gus slowed down. His eyelids became heavy. He nestled into a little snow bank, and with

a smile as big as the sky, Gus drifted off to sleep.

Suddenly, he sat up. "What was that? I know I heard something. Hmmm. Maybe it's the one who made me and gave me my joy. Good! I can finally say thank you for this fine cap and handsome vest!"

Gus stood and looked around. Nothing. No one. Then he realized his joy light wasn't glinting off the snow anymore. It was beaming straight ahead at something large, dark, and shadowy. The forest! Its towering, jagged treetops looked like they were pinned here and there to the sky itself. It looked like a huge curtain, darker even than the night. Gus stared. His joy light seemed to cut an opening into that awful, scary curtain. And Gus could see inside!

"No happy, dancing snowflakes anywhere! But maybe someone needs my light. Maybe my maker is in there somewhere." After a long pause, he whispered to himself, "I need to go in."

Gus mustered up his courage. He walked over and picked up his hat. After brushing it off, he put it back on his head. With his eyes on the trees, Gus put his chin up and his shoulders back. He yelled, "Onward!" Guided by the joy light, he made his way slowly but steadily toward the forest, not knowing what to expect.

CHAPTER 2
The Meeting

The forest trees stood very close together. Gus ducked down and crawled through a gap under some pine branches. He squished his toes into the spongy, damp cushion of dead leaves and pine needles that covered the forest floor. It smelled moldy. He already missed his fresh, clean, crisp snowy field.

Gus climbed across fallen logs, tripped over sticks and squeezed through sticker bushes. "How does anybody get around in here?"

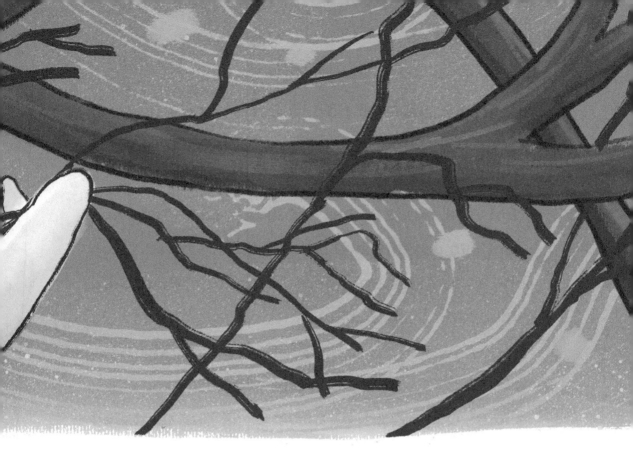

Gus stopped. He turned and looked hard in every direction. "I think I went too far. I never meant to go this deep into the woods. I don't know where I am anymore!" The towering trees completely hid the sky. Their tall, dark trunks stood like giants, blocking his way. Branches swayed and moaned in the wind. A cold chill ran up Gus's spine.

"Oh, why didn't I bring some of those snowballs to drop along the way to mark my path? It's too late now. What if I can't find my way back? I'll never see my snowy field again!" Gus started to run. He tripped over a large tree root and splat! He fell flat on his face. "Boo hoo hoo!" He cried into the dark, lonely night, "Boo hoo hoo!" After a moment, he heard, "Whoo whoo whoo? Whoo whoo whoo?"

Gus looked up and found himself face-to-face with an enormous owl. The bird stood like a king, wearing a long brown cloak that feathered out into the darkness. His broad, flat face and deep yellow eyes made Gus shake with fear. Smaller animals crawled around in the shadows behind the owl.

"These must be his servants," Gus thought, "What have I gotten myself into?"

Looking down at Gus with a nasty glare, the bird spoke, "I am the Great Horned Owl. I reign over the night forest. You don't belong here. Your light bothers my eyes. Snuff it out right now."

"Oh, but Great Horned Owl, this light guided

me here." Gus pulled open his vest and leaned
up to show off his light.

The owl squinted and turned away. "That
small light of yours is no good here. What do you
think you're going to do with it?"

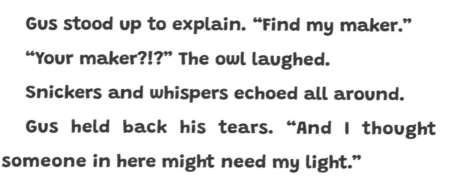

Gus stood up to explain. "Find my maker."

"Your maker?!?" The owl laughed.

Snickers and whispers echoed all around.

Gus held back his tears. "And I thought someone in here might need my light."

"No one in here needs or wants your light!"

"You don't understand! I was just a snowman..."

"You still are *just* a snowman!" The owl screeched.

A raccoon jumped down from a branch. "BOO!"

Gus lost his balance and fell backward onto a thorn bush. "Ouch!" He cried.

Laughter shot out of the darkness, hitting Gus like darts. The whole forest seemed to be making fun of him.

"Listen, snowman!" The owl swooped over the thorn bush. "Take that light and go back where you came from, or you'll be in for some *real* trouble in these woods!"

At that, he spread his wings and flew off into the night. Gus stared after him in wonder. He could see why the Great Horned Owl was king. He pulled himself out of the thorn bush and looked around. The night was quiet, and he was alone once again.

CHAPTER 3
Gus Makes a Friend

Poor Gus. His trip to the forest was supposed to be a grand adventure. Now here he was, full of thorns and lost. The only thing to do was find a comfortable tree stump. He sat down, pulled out thorns, and started to think.

"That owl is right. I am just a snowman. I don't belong here. If I had never come alive, I wouldn't be feeling these thorns and I wouldn't be in this mess."

Gus heard a very soft voice say something. He turned his head to listen. Nothing. Wait! There it was again. He pulled out one last thorn and got up to check. It was coming from a honeysuckle bush.

"Pssst! Hey!" the voice whispered. "Are they gone?"

Gus bent down for a closer look.

"Who? Oh! The owl and his followers? Yes! Yes, I think they're all gone."

"Well then, hurry up! Climb on down! Fast! They don't know I live here!"

Gus shimmied under the bush until he reached the opening of a short tunnel. He put his face over the hole and peered in. A bunny rabbit in thick, blue-rimmed glasses and a polka-dotted apron was at the bottom, looking up at him.

"Who are you?" Gus yelled down.

"Shhh! Lisa Lottie," she whispered. "Just call me Lottie. Now let's go!" She motioned for him to follow her inside.

Gus squeezed down into the burrow. It wasn't as dark as he had expected. A little stone fireplace sat in one corner, with a steaming copper tea kettle resting on its tiny fire. Gus spotted a comfy-looking couch, but the rabbit pushed him into a chair before he could reach it.

"This is big! This is a really big deal! We haven't had light up in the forest since that owl took over. My Uncle Chester and a brave troop of chipmunks tried to stop him, but the owl had them all arrested and taken away. No one knows where. But now... you and your light! You're *here*!"

Gus felt terrifically important. He leaned back, straightened up, and put his hands on his knees. He told Lottie the whole story of coming alive and being led into the forest by his joylight.

Lottie leaned in. "How can I get a joylight to shine out of *my* heart?"

"Well," Gus stood up and rubbed his chin, "mine is made out of little field stones. Do you have anything ordinary lying around we could use?"

Lottie jumped up and grabbed an old tin button box from her shelf. She opened the lid and dumped out all kinds of buttons on the floor.

They both got down on their knees and searched through them. There were tiny ones that looked like pink rosebuds and others were flat and yellow like the sun. Some were a foggy kind of clear, like ice on a pond. Gus handed the buttons to Lottie and she sewed them onto her apron one by one, spelling

J-O-Y right over her heart.

Oh, the light that shone from that little burrow! There was nothing else like it on that cold dark night in the woods. Lottie opened her arms and spun in circles. "Gus, I think everything's going to be okay. For the first time in my life, I have hope."

"Oh, I know what you mean! Isn't it great?"

"Gus, I've never talked to a snowman before. None ever came through these parts. But if they're all like you, the land of snow must be quite a place. Quite a place indeed!"

Lottie stopped twirling and smiled at Gus. She handed him a bag of maple-mint marvels she had

baked that morning and said tenderly, "Keep going, Gus. Trust your light."

Their eyes met. The hopeful look that shone through the thickness of her glasses told Gus that Lottie was counting on him.

"I will," said Gus.

"Until we meet again then." She dabbed her eyes with the corner of her apron.

Gus waved goodbye and then squiggled his way back up to the top of the ground.

"Hey, Lottie?" he called back down, "You're my first friend. I won't forget you!"

"I won't forget you either, Gus."

He crawled out from under the honeysuckle bush and looked around for a moment. There was a faint noise, like a *tat-a-tat*, over and over again. He decided it was as good a reason as any to choose a direction. And Gus followed the sound.

CHAPTER 4
Things Aren't Always
What They Seem

"I 've got a heart full of light, a belly full of cookies and a real friend. What more could I want? Hmmm, maybe a nap." After finding a comfortable looking, moss-covered rock in front of a large tree, he nestled down. Soon he was sound asleep and pleasantly snoring.

A sleek red fox stepped out from behind the same tree where Gus was sleeping.

"Is that him?" he whispered.

"Yep, Sax, that's him alright," replied his cousin Max.

Max and Sax were a couple of handsome foxes.

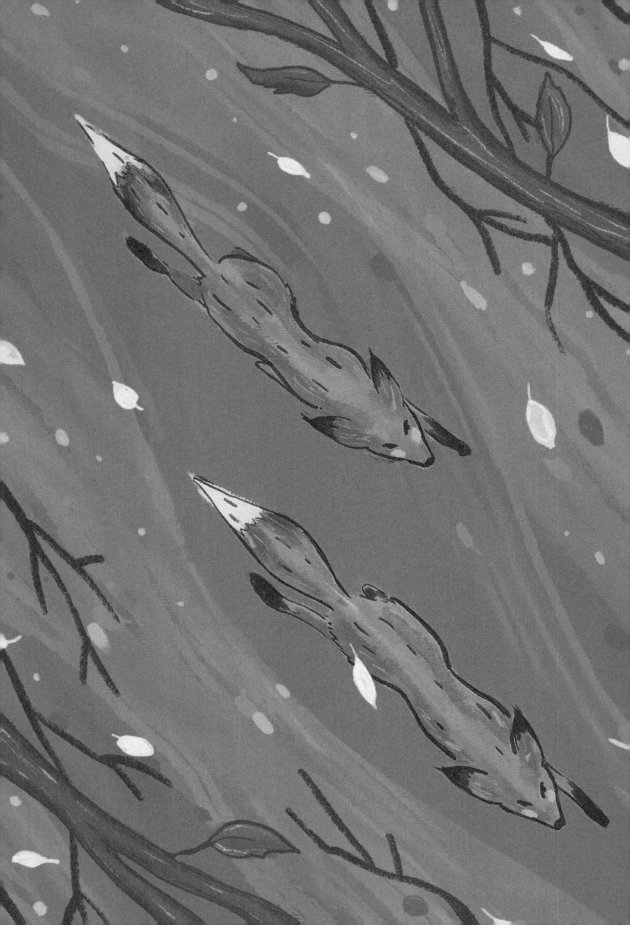

They had long, lush fur and their bushy tails looked like fat, red paint brushes dipped in thick, white paint. Oh, the two of them sure were something! They had tricked many simple forest animals with their beauty. And here they were, leaning over Gus, watching him sleep, and waiting to set their trap.

"Look at that smile. What do you think our little snowman's dreaming about, Max?"

"Snow, I guess."

Sax bent down close to Gus's face. "So peaceful. It seems such a shame to—"

Tat-a-tat! Tat tat tat! Tat-a-tat! Tat tat tat!

Max and Sax jumped backward. "What's going on?!" Max whispered.

Tat-a-tat! Tat tat tat! Tat-a-tat! Tat tat tat!

"There it goes again!" Sax cried. "He's waking up! Let's get out of here! We'll trap him later!" The foxes ran away.

Gus rubbed his eyes. He felt great. A good nap was just what he needed.

Tat-a-tat! Tat tat tat! Tat-a-tat! Tat tat tat!

He stood up and wandered toward the sound. After a while, he stepped out into a small clearing littered with piles of sawdust. He spotted a woodpecker high up on a blue spruce tree. He was wearing a brown leather utility belt, and several tools were hanging from it. His head vibrated so hard in a steady riveting motion that Gus couldn't even tell what color it was.

"Hello up there! What're you doing?"

No response, just more *Tata-tats*! Gus cupped his hands around his mouth and yelled,

"HEY UP THERE! WHAT'RE YOU DOING?!?"

The *tata-tat* stopped. A rather annoyed, ruffled, red head looked down and called,

"My job! Hey, are you a *snowman*?"

"Yes... yes, I am. My name's Gus."

The woodpecker shimmied down the tree with his work belt. He kept shaking his head and looking over his shoulder at Gus as if he were expecting him to disappear. Gus was shaking his head too, but for quite a different reason.

"How can you possibly think with all that racket?" Gus asked.

Finally on the ground, the woodpecker answered, "All what racket? And what's there to think about anyway? Stay busy. That's my motto." He eyed Gus from head to toe and grinned. "A couple of the mail pigeons told me they've been to a land where creatures were made out of snow. I never believed 'em! Thought they were pulling my leg. And here I am, talking to a snowman!" He laughed and slapped his knee. "Well, hello Gus, my name's Frank. I'm a contractor. Got myself a good little business. Made most of the bird condos in these parts. Just finished those red roofed beauties you passed on your way here."

Gus didn't remember seeing anything with a red roof and had no idea what a bird condo was. So, he just nodded and smiled politely. Then he sat down

on a rock to talk with Frank.

"So, Gus, what brings you to my neck of the woods?" Frank opened his toolbox and pulled out a sandwich.

"Well, I wanted to see what all the noise was about. And my joy light! I was looking for someone who might need it."

"You've come to the right place!" Frank opened

some snacks. "Chips?"

"Uh... sure!"

Frank closed his toolbox and sat down on it. Gus helped himself to lots of chips while Frank ate his sandwich and they talked.

"That light of yours would make a nifty headlamp. I could work much longer if I didn't have to depend on moonlight or starlight." They both looked up at the cloudy sky. Frank had a point. "How much do you want for it? I'll make you a good deal." Frank couldn't take his eyes off the light; it was beaming out of every buttonhole in Gus's vest.

"Gee Frank... it's not for your *head*, it's for your *heart*."

"Whatever. How much do you want?"

Gus shook his head and said, "It's not for sale, Frank. It's free. But it only works in your heart."

Frank was on his feet now, "Sounds like faulty wiring to me. A light like that can't be of much value. Tell you what I'll do. You leave the light with me. I'll fix it."

"Sorry, Frank. That's just not how it goes. You have to want it for your heart or it won't shine at all." Gus stood up and put his hands on his hips.

Frank was on his feet now. He stared hard at Gus. He wanted that light. He put all the trash back in his toolbox, snapped it shut and scratched his head. "Too bad. That light sure could be useful to me. Well, I have to get back to work now."

"Okay, Frank. It was nice meeting you. Any idea what would be a good direction to follow? I'm also in these woods to try and find my maker."

Frank looked down and shuffled his feet in the dirt. "Look, Gus. Things in this forest aren't always what they seem. I stay busy. Best way to keep out of trouble. My advice to you is go back the way you came. I'd hate to see something happen..." Frank's voice sort of trailed off while he climbed back up his tree.

Gus wanted to ask him if he was afraid of the Great Horned Owl, but decided to just go.

After he walked a short way, he heard Frank yell

from the tree, "If you change your mind about that light, you know where to find me!"

Gus just sighed and smiled. He liked Frank and wanted to see him again someday.

He mumbled to himself, "I can't go back. Lottie's counting on me to go forward. And what if that owl is still back there waiting for me?" Gus shivered at the thought.

Actually, Gus knew he couldn't go back, even if he wanted to. He never marked his trail, and every spot in the woods looked exactly the same to him as the last spot he was in. With nothing else to do, Gus just chose a direction and kept walking. Finally, his joy light guided him on to an even path.

CHAPTER 5

Jumped from Behind

HA-HA

HE-HE

The *tata-tat-ing* became softer and more distant as Gus walked on. He didn't know if he should be scared or excited about what might happen next. One thing for sure, he felt hungry again. After a bit, his light caught a glimpse of some berry bushes on the side of the path.

"Oh boy! Those look good. I wonder if the berry juice will stain—"

All of a sudden—WHOMP!

"Ahhh! Who's on my back? Get off my head!"

WHOMP! WHOMP! WHOMP! With each whomp, another animal jumped on Gus. The air filled with a high-pitched screechy kind of sound. And the whomps kept coming.

Gus panicked and started spinning in circles, trying to throw off the animals. But all he did was lose his balance and fall flat on his face right into the berry bushes. The

berries smashed, and yes, they *did* stain. Small splotches covered his hat and vest. His snow? Well, it looked like he had the measles. Gus struggled to free himself, but he only got more tangled in the berry bushes.

"Oh! Oh my!" He twisted around and saw his attackers: a small gang of chipmunks. Balls of striped fur were rolling on the ground, pointing at him and laughing.

"How dare you! Oh! You are all so bad!" The more flustered Gus became, the more they doubled over in laughter.

The smallest chipmunk was swinging upside down on a low tree branch above the bushes. With each swing, she grabbed more berries and stuffed them in her mouth. She couldn't have cared less about Gus's predicament. She tossed every berry she thought wasn't ripe back down on his head, even while he was yelling.

He finally climbed out of the bushes and brushed himself off. "Listen you... you little... animals! It's nighttime! You should all be sleeping, not playing tricks! Look at me! I'm polka-dotted!"

One of the taller ones finally stepped forward. "We're sorry. At first we didn't even think you were

real. Then Jack said..."

"Wait a minute!" Jack pushed forward. "*I'm* not the one who started this! Ronald did!"

"Me?" Ronald whined, "Who's the one who said, 'There's only one way to find out!'?"

They all shrugged and looked around at each other.

"That would be me!" the smallest one giggled, munching the berries. Anyone could tell she was very proud of herself. Still hanging from her branch, covered in berry juice, she couldn't stop laughing.

Everyone but Gus thought this was very funny. If snowmen could turn red with anger, Gus would have been as red as a ripe tomato.

"That's enough! Time to make our new friend feel welcome." A scruffy little chipmunk in a torn blue tee shirt strolled toward Gus. He held out his paw for Gus to shake. "My name's Mike. I kinda run the show around here, and these are my younger brothers: Jack, Jerry, Buddy and Ronald. That little nut who put the nasty blotch on your forehead is

our baby sister, Lucy."

Lucy let out a half-hearted "Sorrrrryyy." She jumped down from her perch, still smiling and drinking in every drop of fun from the situation.

The chipmunks sat down and listened to Mike. He continued, "We've been on our own for a while now. Our parents... well, they've gone missing. They had a run-in with the Great One. He's the great horned owl who became king of the forest. One night he sent two wolves to bring Mom and Dad in for questioning. We haven't seen them since."

"I met him," said Gus.

"You met the Great One?!?" The chipmunks scooted nearer to Gus.

"Yes. I wasn't used to walking in the woods and I fell down." Gus figured there was no need to tell them he was also crying. "And when I looked up, I saw a giant bird staring at me in the most dreadful way."

"Oooooooo!" They huddled closer to Gus, like scouts around a campfire listening to ghost stories.

"I told him I was from a land of snow and—"

Lucy almost jumped out of her skin. "So that place is *real*?" She asked.

"Yes. And one day I came alive and saw that I had this light in my heart. It guided me here to this forest."

"Well, I'll be! You met the Great One and lived
to tell the tale." Mike shook his head and smiled.
They were hanging on every word so tightly that the
slightest crunch of leaves or snapped twigs would
have scared the living daylights out of them.

"Yes, I did."

The chipmunks looked at each other with their
mouths hanging open. They slapped Gus on the

back. He had just gained new status in their eyes.

They all started talking at the same time. "Wooo-eee! Whaddaya know about that? He spoke to the Great One; right to his face! What did he do?"

"Well, he commanded me to cover up my joy light."

"Buddy told me that was a flashlight you were carrying in an inside pocket." Lucy yelled and made a face at Buddy.

"A flashlight? No sirreee!" Gus patted his light. "Not a flashlight and not a headlamp, either."

"Headlamp?" Someone called out.

"Never mind. I'll show you."

Gus opened his vest. He surprised himself with what he saw. The word JOY was formed perfectly by the loveliest stones anyone anywhere has ever seen. Each was its own dazzling shade of green, gold, red, blue, purple, or white. They looked far prettier than even the most colorful stones in the clear water of a stream on a sunny day. These stones were like stars, able to hold back the night

itself.

"That looks like a light that could find anything... anyone... anywhere," Mike gasped.

"But they were just ordinary stones! I'm sure of it!" Now it was Gus's turn to have his mouth hang wide open. He looked at the little chipmunks and said, "I don't know if this light will find your parents, but if you want it for your own heart, it will lead you through the darkness of night. It will stay with you like a friend, until the morning."

"Well, boys," Mike asked, "Are you game?"

"YES!"

"Lucy?"

"Yep! We want it too."

"Okay, Gus. What do we do?"

"Well, let's gather up whatever we can—whether it's dirty, broken, old—doesn't matter."

They emptied their pockets. There was quite a variety of old bugs, nuts, dried berries, twigs, dead leaves, and so on. Buddy and Jack dug up some dirt and used spit to make a paste with it so their collection of things would stick. Gus helped them spell J-O-Y on their fur, right over their hearts.

Suddenly it was as though large searchlights

were crisscrossing the night sky; only these were
much brighter. The chipmunks jumped and bounced
off each other for sheer joy. It was a wonderful
sight! A beautiful, happy sight. In fact, they were
so delighted with their new gift they forgot to say
thank you or even goodbye to Gus. They danced

through the trees and kept going until they were deep into the woods.

For quite a while, Gus stood there staring after them. Their lights were beaming all over the place. Then, they must have turned a corner somewhere, and could no longer be seen. Gus smiled. "Oh, I hope the light wasn't wasted on that silly bunch. Though I do want them to find their parents. They sure could use a regular bedtime." Gus shook his head slowly and walked away. He did not yet realize that the joy light is never wasted on anyone.

All that joy made Gus completely forget about the owl and his threats.

"The forest isn't such a bad place." Gus told himself. He turned and looked back down the path he had taken. Thoughts of Lottie, Frank, and those silly chipmunks filled his eyes with happy tears. He was so glad to have shared his light.

Now Gus's joylight beamed in a brand new direction. He had no idea about the adventures waiting for him. But filled with fresh hope, he said, "I must keep going. I feel like there's something I need to do, someone I have to meet. And besides, I haven't found my maker yet."

And just like he did when he first entered the forest, Gus put his chin up in the air, called out, "Onward!" and followed the joylight.

(or is it just the
beginning?)

About the Author

Cheryl, a retired elementary school teacher residing in Baltimore, Maryland, shares her life with Harold, her husband and best friend. Together, they have created a warm and loving home, which they also share with JJ, a lovable rescue lab who has stolen their hearts. Cheryl's passion for storytelling has captivated others throughout the years, and she has finally decided to put one of her tales into writing. The book, titled "Gus and the Joylight," holds a special place in Cheryl's heart, as it represents a lifelong journey of imagination and discovery.

Growing up in a large house with siblings who were much older, Cheryl often found herself yearning for adventure. While they were off exploring the world, she discovered that her imagination was her own personal gateway to new and exciting places. Later, this realization stayed with her as she embarked on her own journeys across the United States and various other countries. What she learned along the way was that a journey is never truly over; it always leads to something more, just like the story of Gus.

About Inklet Press

Inklet Press, a publishing company located in Maryland, USA, aims to support adults in their literary journey by fostering their creative writing abilities. The publisher draws inspiration from *The Inklings*, a renowned creative writing club that existed from the 1930s to the 1940s and included notable figures such as C.S. Lewis, J.R.R. Tolkien, Charles Williams, and Owen Barfield. *The Inklings* were a group of passionate individuals who emphasized the significance of storytelling in fiction and encouraged the exploration of fantasy genres.

In a similar vein, the members of *The Inklets,* a creative writing club formed just before the start of the 2020-2022 period, found solace and camaraderie during the challenging times of the pandemic through their regular writing gatherings. As they produced an array of poems and literary works during these meetings, they decided to venture into publishing some of their creations.

Stay updated on *Inklet Press'* latest releases and ***The Joylight Series (Gus series)*** by following them on Instagram (**@inkletpress**) and visiting their website (**inkletpress.com).**

We are thrilled to announce that
this is the inaugural book in an
incredible trilogy! Stay connected
with us on Instagram at

@inkletpress

for all the latest updates on our
upcoming books. Join us on this
exhilarating journey!

Made in the USA
Columbia, SC
15 August 2024

40025272R00043